Pocket Scientist
FUN WITH ELECTRONICS

J. G. McPherson

Illustrated by Colin King

Remi Chin

5.5.90

Editor: Lisa Watts

Contents

Electronics consultant: Martin Owen
Technical advice by Jaqo
Lettering and circuit diagrams by J. G. McPherson

First published in 1981 by
Usborne Publishing Ltd,
20 Garrick Street,
London WC2E 9BJ, England
Copyright © 1981
Usborne Publishing Ltd
Published in Australia by
Rigby Publishing Ltd, Adelaide,
Sydney, Melbourne, Brisbane.

About this book

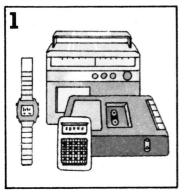

Electronics is the very careful and precise control of tiny electric currents. Digital watches, transistor radios, calculators, tape recorders and computers all work by means of electronics.

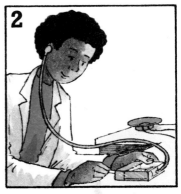

This book shows you how to build lots of electronic things, using the electric current from a battery. Over the page you can find out about the things you need, and you can find out where to buy them on page 60.

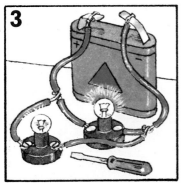

On the next few pages there are some tests you can do to find out how electronics works. Then there are some general instructions showing you how to build electronic equipment. You need to read these instructions before you tackle the projects.

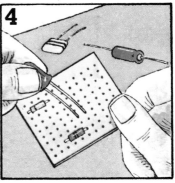

When you are building electronic things you have to be very careful and accurate. If one tiny thing is in the wrong place, the project will not work. Do not worry, though, if your projects do not work at first. There is a checklist to help you find the faults on page 64.

Things you need

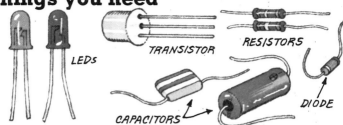

LEDs

TRANSISTOR

RESISTORS

CAPACITORS

DIODE

To build the projects you need tiny things called electronic components. They are very small and cheap and you can find out where to get them at the bottom of the page.

The components control the current in various ways, and you will find out more about them as you read through the book.

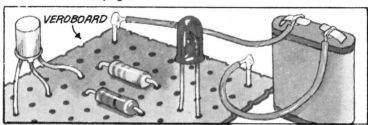

VEROBOARD

For each project you have to connect the components together in a certain way, called a circuit. The way the current flows through the circuit is what makes the project work.

To build a circuit you solder the components to special board called Veroboard. You can find out how to do this, and how to solder, in the general instructions later in the book.

Buying components and board

You can buy components and Veroboard at electronics components shops. If there is no shop near you, you can write to a supplier and ask them to send you the things you need.

There is more advice about buying components on page 60, and a complete list of the components you need for all the projects and tests in this book.

Tools

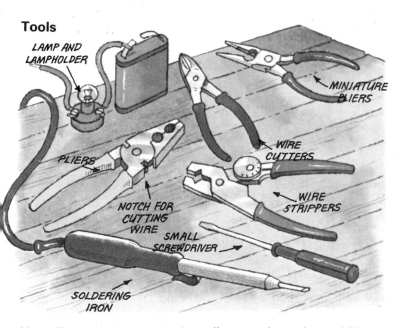

LAMP AND LAMPHOLDER

MINIATURE PLIERS

PLIERS

WIRE CUTTERS

NOTCH FOR CUTTING WIRE

WIRE STRIPPERS

SMALL SCREWDRIVER

SOLDERING IRON

You will need a very small screwdriver and a pair of miniature pliers. Wire strippers are useful for taking the plastic cover off wires, but you can use pliers or scissors instead. You also need a pair of wire cutters, or ordinary pliers which have a wire cutter on the side, and a soldering iron.

Battery power

NEVER USE THE ELECTRICITY IN YOUR HOUSE FOR THE PROJECTS. THE CURRENT IS MUCH TOO STRONG AND IT WOULD GIVE YOU A VERY BAD SHOCK AND COULD EVEN KILL YOU.

All the projects in this book work on the electric current from a battery. Never connect any of the projects to the electricity in the plugs in your house. The current from these plugs is much too strong and it would burn out all the components in the project.

5

How electronics works

An electric current is created by a flow of minute particles called electrons. Electronic equipment works by controlling and using these electrons.

Electrons are part of the atoms of which everything in the world is made. This book and everything else around you is made of millions of invisibly small atoms.

NUCLEUS

ELECTRONS

There are lots of different kinds of atoms, and every atom has a nucleus in the middle, with electrons spinning round it.

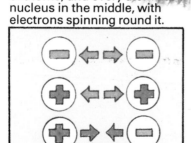

Charges of positive and negative electricity are attracted to each other, and charges which are the same (e.g. two negative charges), move away from each other.

Each electron carries a tiny bit of electricity called a negative charge. The nucleus has a positive charge of electricity.

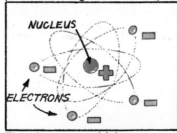

NUCLEUS

ELECTRONS

The electrons, which are negatively charged, usually stay spinning round the nucleus because they are attracted by the positive charge of the nucleus.

Making current

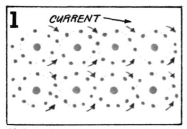

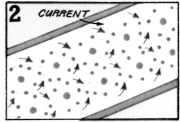

If there is a stronger positive charge nearby, the electrons in some substances will leave their nuclei and flow towards the stronger positive charge. This flow of electrons creates an electric current. The electrons in metals move easily, and metals are said to be good conductors of electricity. Electrons in plastic do not move, so electric current cannot flow through plastic.*

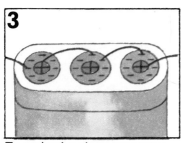

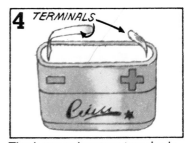

To make the electrons move you can use a battery. The battery contains a supply of strong positive and negative electric charges.

The battery has two terminals. One terminal is connected to the positively charged part of the battery and the other to the negatively charged part.

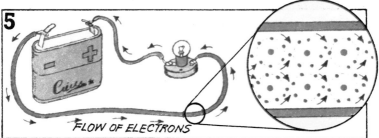

If you connect a piece of wire to the positive and negative battery terminals, the electrons in the wire will flow towards the positive charge in the battery. In this picture the wires are also connected to a bulb. The bulb lights up and this shows that the movement of the electrons is an electric current.

*This is why electric wires are made of metal covered with plastic. 7

Batteries, wire and lamps

This page shows the batteries, wire and lamps you can use.
Opposite, you can find out how to fix wire to batteries.

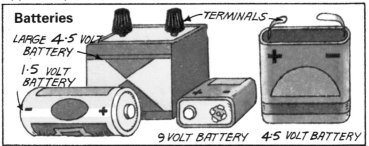

Batteries

TERMINALS

LARGE 4·5 VOLT BATTERY

1·5 VOLT BATTERY

9 VOLT BATTERY

4·5 VOLT BATTERY

The force in the battery which makes the electrons move is called the voltage, and the strength of the battery is measured in volts. Some of the projects in this book need a 4.5 volt battery and others need a 9 volt battery.

Batteries come in lots of shapes and sizes and there are several different types of terminals. It does not matter which you use as long as it is the right voltage.

Electric wire

SOLID CORE

STRANDED

TWIN CABLE

This has a core of metal, to carry the electric current, covered with a plastic case. Some electric wire has a solid core of metal, others have strands of metal inside. It does not matter which you buy, but thin wire, such as "bell wire" and seven stranded wire, is easiest to use. If you have "twin cable", split it by cutting the case between the wires, then pulling the wires apart.

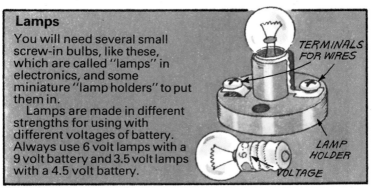

Lamps

You will need several small screw-in bulbs, like these, which are called "lamps" in electronics, and some miniature "lamp holders" to put them in.

Lamps are made in different strengths for using with different voltages of battery. Always use 6 volt lamps with a 9 volt battery and 3.5 volt lamps with a 4.5 volt battery.

TERMINALS FOR WIRES

LAMP HOLDER

VOLTAGE

Stripping wire

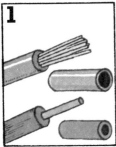

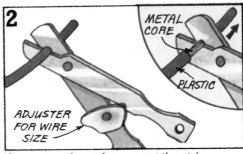

You have to remove 1.5cm of the plastic from each end of a piece of wire.

If you use wire strippers, set the strippers so they cut through the plastic, but not through the metal core. Grip the wire in the strippers, about 1.5cm from the end, and firmly pull the plastic case off the metal.

If you are careful, you can strip wire with scissors. Grip the wire in the scissors and twist, so the scissors score the plastic. Then pull the plastic off.

Fixing wire to batteries

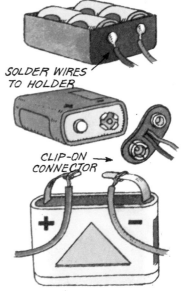

SOLDER WIRES TO HOLDER

CLIP-ON CONNECTOR

These pictures show how to fix wires to the various types of terminals on batteries. If you use stranded wire, twist the strands together in your fingers, so the wire is easier to handle.

If you use round batteries, you will need a battery holder to put them in. You can buy one, or take one out of an old radio. You can also use sticky tape to hold batteries and wires together.

Battery and lamp experiments

Here are some experiments you can do with a battery and lamps to find out more about how current flows. You need a 4.5 volt battery, two 3.5 volt lamps, two lamp holders and two pieces of wire about 25cm long. Before you start, strip the plastic case off the ends of the wires, as shown on the previous page.

1

TERMINALS

Twist one end of each wire firmly round the battery terminals.

2

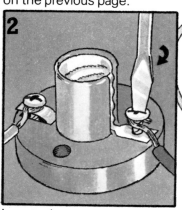

Loosen the screws on the lamp holder and twist the other ends of the wires clockwise round the screws. Tighten the screws.

3

Now screw a lamp into the lamp holder. If it does not light up, check that the wires are firmly connected to the battery and lamp holder.

4

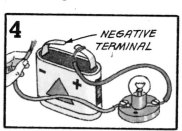

NEGATIVE TERMINAL

Try taking the wire off the negative battery terminal. The lamp goes out. This shows that the positive charge by itself cannot make the electrons move.

5

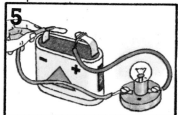

Now touch the negative terminal with the wire again. For current to flow there has to be a complete link, called a circuit, from the negative to the positive part of the battery.

How lamps work

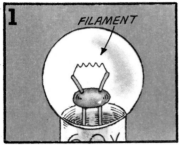

Inside a lamp there is a very thin wire called a filament, through which the electric current has to pass. The filament is so thin that it is difficult for all the electrons to flow through it.

As the electrons squeeze through the filament, the wire becomes white hot and gives off light. The way the wire restricts the flow of electrons is called resistance.

Another experiment

Now try setting up a battery like this, with two 3.5 volt lamps linked by a piece of wire. What happens to the light from the lamps this time?

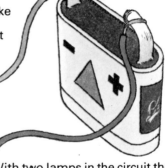

With two lamps in the circuit there is twice as much resistance to the flow of electrons as there was with only one lamp. This reduces the amount of current in the wires, so the lamps are dimmer.

Measures of electricity

The force in the battery which makes the electrons move is called the **voltage.** It is measured in **volts,** written **V** for short.

The amount of current that flows through the wires is measured in **amperes,** written **amps** or **A** for short.

The amount of resistance to the flow of electrons is measured in **ohms,** written Ω for short.* $K\Omega$ is used for 1,000 ohms.

*Ω is the sign for the Greek letter omega.

Circuit diagrams

A circuit diagram is a drawing which shows how the components in a circuit are connected. Each component is shown by a symbol. The symbols for lamps, batteries and wires are shown here, and there are also some simple circuits to build.

The circuit diagrams for the projects in this book are on pages 58–59. You do not have to use the diagrams, though, to build the projects.

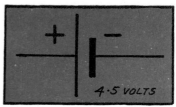

This is the symbol for a battery. The thin line is the positive (+ve) terminal and the shorter, thicker one is the negative (−ve) terminal. The strength of the battery is written beside the symbol.

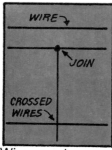

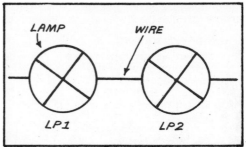

Wires are shown as straight lines and a dot shows where wires are joined.

Lamps are shown like this, with the straight lines between them showing the wires. Each of the components in a circuit is labelled with its initial and number.

Circuit diagram

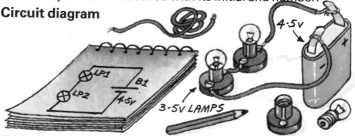

This is the diagram for the lamps and battery circuit shown here. When the lamps are placed like this, one after the other on the same piece of wire, it is called a "series circuit". Try building the circuit, then unscrew one of the lamps. This makes a break in the circuit so the other lamp goes out as it is no longer linked to both the battery terminals.

More circuits to build

See if you can build the circuits shown below, following the diagrams.

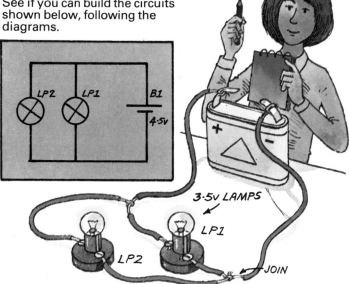

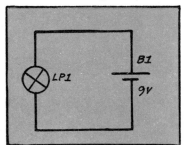

This circuit has two lamps on separate loops of wire. It is called a "parallel circuit". Try undoing one of the lamps. The other lamp stays alight as there is still a complete circuit to and from the battery. The lamps in this circuit are brighter than those in the series circuit because the same amount of current from the battery flows along each loop of wire. In the series circuit, both the lamps are resisting the current on the same piece of wire, so they both receive less current.

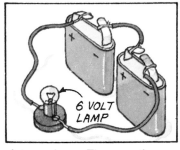

This diagram shows that the circuit needs a 9 volt battery. If you do not have one you can link two 4.5 volt batteries in a series circuit as shown in the picture above. The negative terminal of one battery should be linked to the positive terminal of the other battery.

13

Electronic components

These two pages show the electronic components you will be using to build the projects. You can find out more about them on pages 48-55, and there are also some tests to show how they work. It is a good idea to do some of the tests before you build the projects, so you get used to handling the components and can see how they work.

The components you buy may not look exactly the same as the ones shown here and in the projects, as there are lots of different kinds which do the same job. On pages 62-63 there are some clues to help you sort out your components for the projects.

Resistors

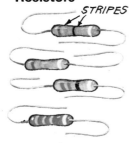

STRIPES

These reduce the amount of current in the circuit by resisting the flow of the electricity. The strength of each resistor, that is, its resistance, is measured in ohms (written Ω, or KΩ for 1,000 ohms). The resistance is marked on each resistor with a code of coloured stripes. In the projects, resistors are referred to by the colours of their stripes. You can find out how to read the colours at the bottom of the opposite page and the code is explained on page 49.

Variable resistors

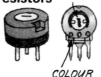

SCREW

COLOUR CODE

These are another kind of resistor. By turning the screw in the middle (with a very small screwdriver, or penknife) you can vary the amount by which they reduce the current. Some variable resistors have their maximum resistance marked on them in numbers of ohms. Others have three coloured dots from the resistor colour code.

Diodes

Diodes are rather like one-way streets – the current can flow through them one way but not the other. You have to be careful to connect them correctly and there is a stripe on one end of the diode to show you how.

Light emitting diodes or LEDs

FLAT EDGE

These glow like tiny bulbs and, like diodes, the current can only flow through them one way. The base of the case of an LED has a flat edge to help you identify the legs. You have to look carefully to see it. The project instructions tell you where to put the leg nearest the flat edge.

Transistors

Transistors can control the strength of the current in the circuit, and can also switch it off and on. You have to be careful to connect transistors correctly as they can be damaged if the current flows through them the wrong way. Each transistor has one leg marked with a coloured spot or metal tag on the case, and the instructions for the projects tell you exactly where to put the legs.

TAG

Capacitors

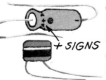

+ *SIGNS*

These components store a small amount of electricity, measured in microfarads (written μF)* or for very small amounts, picofarads (pF). Some capacitors, called "electrolytic capacitors", have + signs on one end and these must be connected the right way in the circuit. The project instructions show you how.

Audio transformer

This changes electric current to make it the best kind of current for a loudspeaker or crystal earpiece.

Other things

YOUR SWITCH AND SOCKET MAY LOOK DIFFERENT FROM THESE

LOUDSPEAKER

CRYSTAL EARPIECE

SWITCH

MINIATURE SOCKET AND PLUG

1 Reading resistor stripes

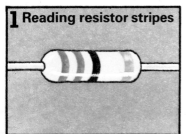

2

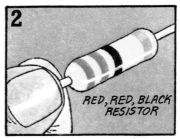

RED, RED, BLACK RESISTOR

Each resistor has three coloured stripes at one end, and a gold, silver, red or brown one near the other end.

To identify a resistor, hold it with the three stripes on the left, then read the colours from left to right. To find out what the colours mean, see page 49.

μ is the sign for the Greek letter "m", called mu.

How to build the projects

To build the projects you connect the components together on special board called Veroboard. This has rows of holes in it, with strips of copper on the back linking the holes. You fit the components through the holes and the electric current flows to them along the copper tracks.

When you buy Veroboard, ask for board with copper strips, and with holes 0.1in apart.

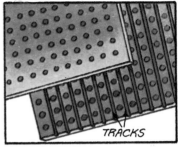

In this book the front of a piece of board is called the "plainside" and the back, with the copper tracks on it, is called the "trackside".

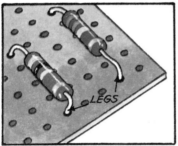

You fit the components through the holes like this, then solder their legs to the tracks. You can find out how to solder over the page.

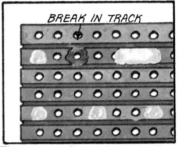

The current flows through all the components soldered to the same track. Sometimes you have to redirect the current by breaking the track.

You can break the track with a drill bit held in your fingers. Use about a 4.5mm bit and turn it to remove all the copper.

To cut board, score it several times on the trackside with a sharp knife (e.g. penknife) and metal ruler. Then break it.

16

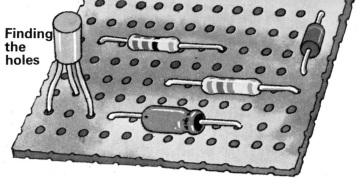

Finding the holes

You have to be very careful to put all the components in the correct holes. In the projects, each hole is called by a letter and number. The letter shows which track it is in and the number shows how many holes it is along the track. Always look at the plainside of the board to count the holes and tracks. To help you find the holes you can draw a grid, as shown below.

Cut the board to the size for the project. The size is given as the number of tracks by the number of holes along a track (e.g. 15 tracks × 21 holes).

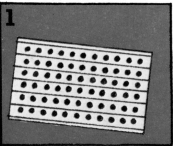

THESE TRACKS ARE VERTICAL

Put the board on a piece of paper with the tracks either horizontal or vertical as indicated in the project. Draw round the board.

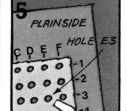

TRACKSIDE

Make marks for the tracks along one edge of the board and for the holes along another edge.

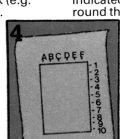

ABCDEF

Then label the tracks with letters (start top left) and the holes with numbers.

PLAINSIDE

HOLE E3

To find a hole put the board, plainside up, on the grid, and read off its letter and number.

How to solder

Soldering is a way of joining two pieces of metal, using melted metal called solder. It makes a firm joint through which the electric current can flow.

When the soldering iron is on, do not touch the bit as it is very hot. Keep the wire of the soldering iron out of your way so there is no danger of burning it with the bit.

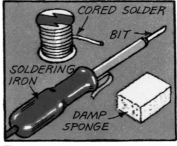

These are the things you will need. "Cored" solder has a substance in it that makes it flow easily when it melts.

Soldering a component

Plug the iron in and wait for it to heat up. Prop it up so the bit is not touching anything.

Find the right holes for the component. You can mark them with a felt-tip pen.

Put the legs of the component through the holes, like this.

Bend the legs out slightly at the back, to hold the component in place.

Wipe the bit on the damp sponge to remove old solder.

Touch the hot bit with solder so a drop clings to it to "wet" it.

Then, both at the same time, put the tip of the solder wire and the bit, on the place where the component's leg touches the track. Leave them there for only about a second, until there is a small amount of solder joining the leg to the track. Then let the joint cool for a few seconds.

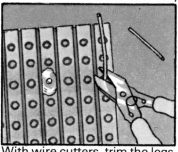

With wire cutters, trim the legs close to the solder. *Tilt the board away from you and put your finger on the leg to stop it flying up out of the cutters.**

REMOVE SOLDER BETWEEN TRACKS AS SHOWN BELOW

The joints should be smooth and shiny and there must not be any solder between the tracks. This would let the current flow from track to track.

To remove solder between tracks, run the hot iron along in the groove.

WHEN YOU HAVE FINISHED SOLDERING REMEMBER TO UNPLUG THE SOLDERING IRON.

If you want to remove a joint, hold the board like this, put the hot iron on the joint and flick the solder towards the table. Be careful as the molten solder is hot.

Be very careful doing this as the pieces of metal can fly a long way. 19

More soldering

1 Wires

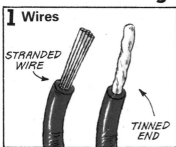

If you use stranded wire you should cover the strands with solder to hold them together. This is called "tinning".

2

TWIST STRANDS TOGETHER

Strip 1cm of the plastic off the wire, then twist the strands together. Put something on the wire to hold it steady while you tin it.

3

CLEAN BIT ON SPONGE

Heat the soldering iron, then clean the bit and "wet" it with solder as before.

4

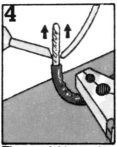

Then quickly stroke the wire with the bit and the solder at the same time.

5

STRANDS SHOWING THROUGH SOLDER

The tinned wire should be lightly coated with solder, like this.

Wire links

LINK BETWEEN TRACKS

Sometimes you need to carry the current from one track to another by linking them with a piece of wire.

SHORT LINK

You can use stranded or solid core wire for links. For very short ones you can use pieces of metal paper clip.

Fixing wires to the board

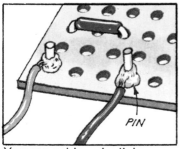

You can solder wire links straight to the track, but other wires should be soldered to pins which are soldered to the board.

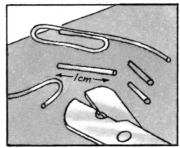

For pins, use pieces about 1cm long cut from metal paper clips, or thick pieces of wire cut off the legs of components.

Fixing pins

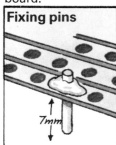

Put the pin in the hole so about 7mm shows on the plainside of board. Solder to track.

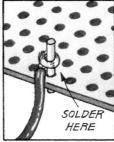

SOLDER HERE

With the board plainside up, wind a piece of wire round the pin, then solder it to the pin.

Hint

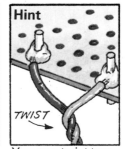

TWIST

You can twist two wires together, like this, to keep them tidy.

Board holder

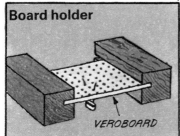

VEROBOARD

Two blocks of wood with grooves in like this, are useful for holding the board while you solder the components.

Clamp the wood in a vice while you saw the grooves. They must be wide enough to take the thickness of the Veroboard.

Hints for success

Before you build any of the circuits it is a good idea to practise soldering some pieces — you will find it much easier after a bit of practice. Make sure you have all the correct components for the project you want to build. There are some clues to help you identify them on page 62. Here are some other points to remember.

1 Remember that the letter for each hole shows which track it is in and the number shows how many holes it is along the track.

2 Take great care to put the legs of the transistors in the correct holes, and to place electrolytic capacitors the right way round.

3 Check each soldered joint (when it is cool) to make sure it is firm and shiny. If it is not, resolder it. Make sure there is no solder between the tracks.

4 Make sure the legs of the components are not touching each other on the plainside.

5 Before you connect the battery, check your board against the project pictures to make sure *all* the components are in the right holes.

6 Make sure you connect the wires from the board to the battery correctly.

7 If the project does not work, turn to the faults checklist at the end of the book. In electronics you often have to check a project several times before you can get it to work.

Boxing the projects

If you like, you can put the projects in boxes. You should decide how you are going to box a project before you build it.*

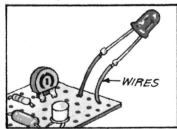

You may need to lengthen the legs of LEDs so they show outside the box. You can do this by soldering pieces of wire to them.

*There are ideas for boxing the projects on pages 56-57.

Things to make
Guessing game

This game has two lights and when you press the switch, one of the lights comes on. You can never tell which one will light up. You could play it with friends, asking them to guess which light will come on, and see who gets it right most often.

GAME IN BOX

VARIABLE RESISTOR

LED

RESISTOR   TRANSISTOR

For hints on identifying the components, see page 62.

Parts list

Two 390Ω* resistors (orange, white, brown)
Two 82KΩ resistors (grey, red, orange)
1KΩ variable resistor (vertical skeleton type)
Two transistors type BC107
Two LEDs
Pushbutton on/off switch
60cm electric wire
Three pins
Veroboard 13 tracks x 15 holes
9 volt battery and clip connector

1 How to build it

TRACKS HORIZONTAL

1 2 3 4

A B C D E F G H I J

Cut the Veroboard to size, put it on a piece of paper with the tracks horizontal and draw a grid (see page 17). Label tracks A–M and number the holes.

2

BREAKS IN TRACKS

Break the track (with a drill bit between your fingers) in holes C3 and E8. Remember to count the holes on the plainside of the board.

*Ω means ohm and KΩ means 1,000 ohm.   23

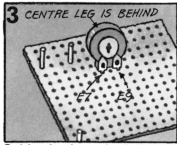

3 CENTRE LEG IS BEHIND

E7 E9

Solder the three pins in holes C1, C4 and M1. Then solder the variable resistor with its centre leg in C8 and the other two in E7 and E9, as above.

4

Solder one of the grey, red, orange resistors (82KΩ) in holes G4, J4, and the other grey, red, orange one in G13, J13. The board should now look like this.

5

Solder the orange, white, brown resistors (390Ω) in holes E2, H2 and E15, H15. Check all the joints so far to make sure they are firm and shiny.

6 NEGATIVE LEGS

The LEDs go in holes H3, J3 and H14, J14. On each, the leg next to the flat edge on the capsule should be in track J.

7

Now break the track in holes G8, H8, J8 and K8.

8 FLAT EDGE

TRACK M

TAGS

One transistor goes in holes J6, K7, M6 and the other in J10, K11, M10. Make sure that on each transistor the leg nearest the metal tag is in track M.

9

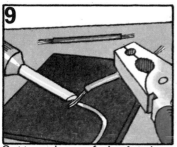

Cut two pieces of wire 4cm long. Strip 0.5cm of the plastic case off each end of both wires. If it is stranded wire, tin the ends with solder, as shown above.

10

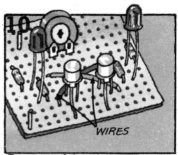

WIRES

Put one of the pieces of wire in holes G5, K12 and the other in K5, G12, so they cross over as in the picture. Solder the wires in position.

11

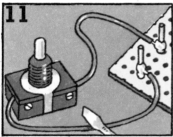

Solder two wires, 8cm long, to pins C1 and C4. Put the other ends of the wires in the holes in the switch and tighten the screws.*

12

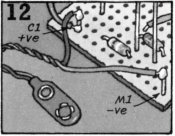

C1 +ve

M1 −ve

Now solder wires for the battery to pins C1 and M1. If you use a clip connector the red wire (positive) must go to C1.

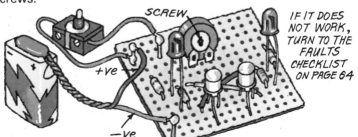

SCREW

+ve

−ve

IF IT DOES NOT WORK, TURN TO THE FAULTS CHECKLIST ON PAGE 64

Then connect the battery and press the switch a few times to test the circuit. If one LED lights up much more often than the other, adjust the variable resistor by turning the screw in the centre with a screwdriver or penknife. Keep adjusting the screw a tiny amount until both LEDs are working.

*If your switch is different from this one, see page 60.

Pot plant tester

You can use this little electronic device to see if a pot plant needs watering. It has only three electronic components and is quite easy to build. The finished board is shown below.

VARIABLE RESISTOR

TRANSISTOR

LED   PROBES

To test a plant you stick the long probes into the earth. If the LED stays on it means the soil is dry and the plant needs watering. If the light flickers, or goes off, the soil is still damp.

Parts list

4.7KΩ variable resistor (vertical skeleton type)
Transistor type BC171A
LED (any colour)
Two pieces of stiff wire 10cm long (you can use straightened paper clips) for the probes
20cm plastic sleeving to cover probes (size 2mm bore) or use sticky tape
20cm electric wire
Two pins
4.5 volt battery
Veroboard 7 tracks x 12 holes

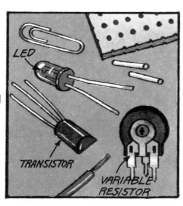

LED

TRANSISTOR

VARIABLE RESISTOR

How to make the pot plant tester

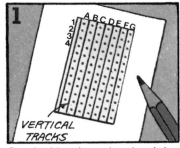

Cut the Veroboard to the right size, then draw a grid with the tracks running vertically. Label the tracks A–G across the top.

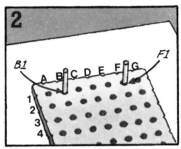

On the plainside of the board, find holes B1 and F1. Put a pin in each of these holes, then turn the board over and solder the pins to the tracks.

Cover the probes with casing or sticky tape, leaving 1cm bare at both ends of each wire.

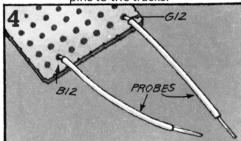

With pliers, bend one end of each probe to make a right angle. Then solder the probes in holes B12 and G12, so they look like this.

The variable resistor goes in holes C5, E4 and E6, with the centre leg in C5. Solder the legs to the back of the board, then break the track in hole E5.

Now solder a short metal link from E7 to F7. You can use a piece of paperclip.

27

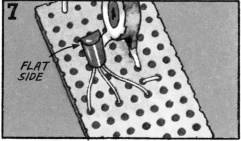

Hold the transistor upright with the flat side facing the variable resistor and put the legs in holes A8, C8 and E8, as shown above. Make sure the flat side is facing the variable resistor.*

Strip the plastic off the ends of a short piece of wire and solder it in holes C9 and G9.

Now examine the LED to find the flat edge on the case (it is hard to see). The leg next to the flat edge is the negative leg. Put the LED in holes A10 and B10, with the negative leg in B10.

Solder the LED to the board then trim off the legs at the back.

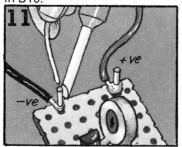

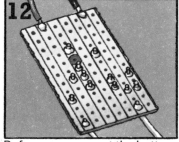

Now solder two 8cm pieces of wire to pins B1 and F1 for the battery. B1 is the negative wire and F1 is the positive wire.

Before you connect the battery, make sure all the pieces are in the right holes and that there is no solder between the tracks.

*If your transistor has a tag, the leg nearest the tag goes in hole A8.

Testing it

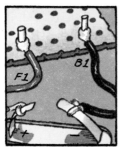

Connect the battery (B1 to negative and F1 to positive). The LED should light up.

Now, if you put the two probes on a piece of damp cloth, the LED should go out. If it stays on, adjust the variable resistor by turning the screw in the centre, until the LED goes out.

How it works

IF IT DOES NOT WORK, TURN TO THE FAULTS CHECKLIST ON PAGE 64

Water is a good conductor of electricity, so when the soil is wet, the current can flow between the two probes. When the current flows this way through the circuit, the

transistor switches off and the LED goes out. When the soil is dry, the current cannot pass between the probes and the LED stays on.

Useful clips

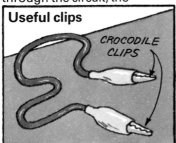

CROCODILE CLIPS

A length of wire with crocodile clips like these on the ends, is useful for connecting a circuit to a battery.

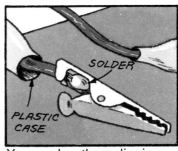

SOLDER

PLASTIC CASE

You can buy these clips in electrical stores, and solder them to a short piece of wire.

How to make a burglar alarm

When this electronic alarm goes off it makes a loud squeaky noise. You could put it on the door of your room, or on a private cupboard, and when someone opens the door, the alarm will go off.

The board with all the components on is shown below.

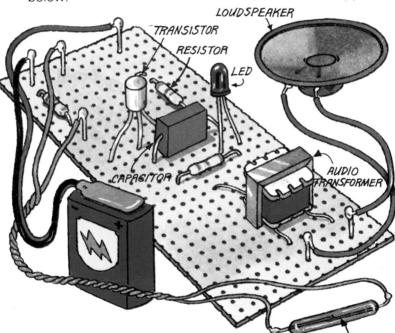

Parts list

22 Ω resistor (red, red, black)
4.7KΩ resistor (yellow, violet, red)
39KΩ resistor (orange, white, orange)
Transistor type AC127
Audio transformer type LT700
0.01μF capacitor *
8Ω miniature loudspeaker
LED (any colour)

Reed switch (normally open type)
Magnet (any kind)
Six pins
9 volt battery and clip connector
Veroboard 14 tracks x 30 holes
Electric wire (enough to reach from the door to where you place the alarm)

* Your capacitor may have brown, black, orange and red stripes.

How to build the alarm

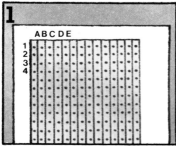

Cut the board to size and draw a grid with the tracks vertical. On the plainside, find the holes B2, E2, K2, B9, H29 and L29. Solder pins in these holes.

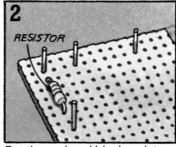

Put the red, red black resistor (22Ω) in holes B3, B7. Then break the track in holes B5, K9, H25 and L25.

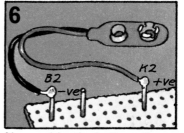

The transistor goes in holes B12, E12 and G12. The leg nearest the spot or tag on the case must go in hole G12.

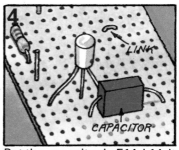

Put the capacitor in E14, L14. It does not matter which leg goes in which hole. Next, solder a wire link from J5 to K5. You can use a piece of paperclip for this.

The yellow, violet, red resistor (4.7KΩ) goes in K6 and K12 and the orange, white, orange one (39KΩ) in E17 and K17.

Now solder the battery clip wires to the pins in B2 and K2. The red wire (positive) must go to K2 and the other wire (negative) to B2.

7

The audio transformer has two thick metal legs. You do not need these, so bend them up flat under it, then solder its wire legs in holes G19, J19, L19, H27 and L27.

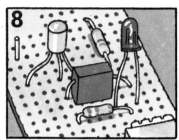

8

Put the LED in J16 and L16. The leg next to the flat edge on the capsule (negative leg) must go in J16.

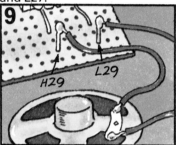

9

Solder two short wires to pins H29 and L29. Then solder the other ends of the wires to the terminals on the back of the loudspeaker.

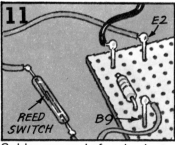

10

Now cut two lengths of wire long enough to reach from the door to where you are going to hide the circuit board and speaker.

11

Solder one end of each wire to each end of the reed switch, and the other ends to pins B9 and E2.

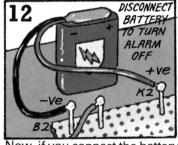

12

Now, if you connect the battery the alarm should go off. B2 is the negative wire and K2 is the positive.

Stick the reed switch on the door frame, very close to the door, using masking tape or insulating tape which will not spoil the paintwork.

Tape the magnet on the door, about 10mm in from the edge, and exactly opposite the reed switch.

HIDE THE WIRE UNDER THE CARPET OR TAPE IT TO THE SKIRTING BOARD

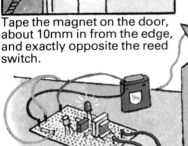

IF IT DOES NOT WORK, TURN TO THE FAULTS CHECKLIST ON PAGE 64

Now connect the battery, then open the door and the alarm should go off. To stop the alarm, close the door or remove the battery. If it does not work, try moving the magnet and reed switch a little bit closer to each other. The circuit is controlled by the reed switch, and the reed switch is operated by the magnet.

This is a bar magnet, but any kind of magnet will do.

33

Shaky hand game

Here is a game you can make to test how steady your hands are. You have to take the handle from one end of the metal loop to the other, without letting it touch the metal. If it does, the buzzer goes off and you are out.

There is a large picture of the finished board with all the components on over the page.

TWIST WIRES TOGETHER TO KEEP THEM TIDY

METAL LOOP

HANDLE

Parts list

22Ω resistor (red, red, black)
4.7KΩ resistor (yellow, violet, red)
27KΩ resistor (red, violet, orange)
Transistor type BFY50
0.22μF capacitor
Audio transformer type LT700
8Ω miniature loudspeaker (you can use the same loudspeaker for all the projects)
LED (any colour)
5 pins
Veroboard 20 tracks x 27 holes
9 volt battery and clip connector

You also need about 1.5m of electric wire to attach to the handle and loudspeaker. The metal loop and handle are made of tinned copper wire. This comes in various thicknesses, so ask for 50cm of s.w.g. (standard wire gauge) 20. You can cover the handle with sticky tape, or buy special plastic sleeving for it. You would need about 12cm of 2mm bore sleeving.

How to build the shaky hand game

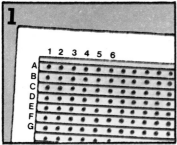

Cut the Veroboard to size and draw a grid with the tracks running horizontally. Label the tracks A–T.

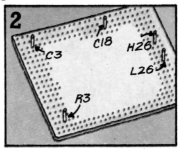

Solder the five pins in holes C3, C18, H26, L26 and R3. Remember to count the holes on the plainside of the board.

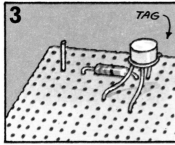

TAG

Fit the red, red, black resistor (22Ω) in C5 and C10 and the transistor in F8, C11 and G11. The leg nearest the tag must be in C11.

PUSH TRANSFORMER DOWN ON TO BOARD

Bend the transformer's thick metal legs up underneath it, then solder its wire legs in holes G19, J19, M19 and H24 and L24.

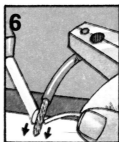

Measure the wire for two links, from C14 to J14 and from J15 to P15.

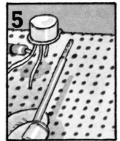

If you use stranded wire, tin the ends before soldering it to the board.*

Solder the wires in position, as shown above.

*For how to "tin", see page 20.

35

Put the yellow, violet, red resistor (4.7KΩ) in P17 and P23, then solder a short wire link from P24 to R24.

The capacitor* goes in M5 and R5 (it does not matter which leg goes in which hole). Then put the red, violet, orange resistor (27KΩ) in R8 and R14.

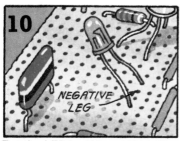

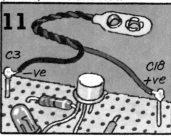

Put the LED in J12 and M12. The negative leg (the one next to the flat edge on the capsule) should be in J12. Break the track in holes C7, C12, P20, R11.

Solder wires for the battery to pins C3 and C18. If you use a battery clip, the black wire (negative) should go to C3, and the red (positive) to C18.

Making the handle

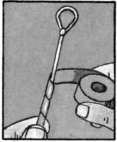

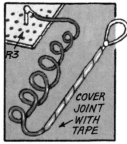

Cut a piece of tinned copper wire 10cm long. Bend the end like this. Solder.

Wind sticky tape round the handle, or cover it with the plastic sleeving.

Solder a piece of wire 1m long to the end of the handle and to pin R3.

*Don't worry if your capacitor looks different from this one.

Making the metal loop

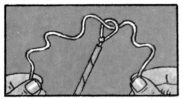

Bend the rest of the tinned copper wire to a shape like this. Then thread the loop of the handle on to it.

TAPE OR SLEEVING

At each end, cover about 2cm of the wire with sticky tape (or sleeving) but leave 1cm bare at the ends, for soldering. Solder the wire in holes F3 and S26.

Loudspeaker

Now solder pieces of wire to pins H26 and L26, and solder the other ends of the wires to the back of the loudspeaker.

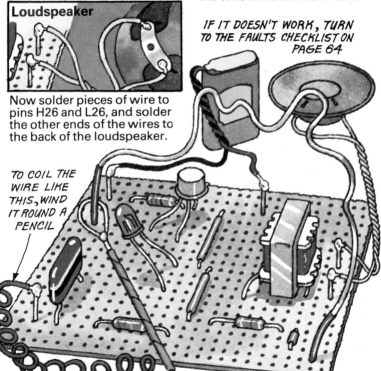

IF IT DOESN'T WORK, TURN TO THE FAULTS CHECKLIST ON PAGE 64

TO COIL THE WIRE LIKE THIS, WIND IT ROUND A PENCIL

Make sure all the pieces are in the right places, then connect the battery. The wire from C3 must go to the negative terminal and the C18 wire to the positive terminal.

Now, when the metal of the handle touches the metal loop, the buzzer should sound.

37

Miniature radio to make

This tiny radio has only two electronic components, and it does not even need a battery. It is small enough to fit in a plastic sweet box, as shown on the right. If you want to box the radio like this, read the instructions at the end of the book before you build it.

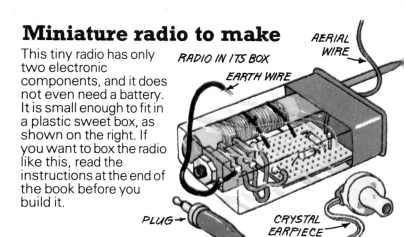

AERIAL WIRE

RADIO IN ITS BOX

EARTH WIRE

PLUG →

CRYSTAL EARPIECE

RADIO OUT OF ITS BOX

TUNING COIL

EARTH WIRE

FERRITE ROD

CAPACITOR

AERIAL WIRE

SOCKET FOR EARPIECE *

DIODE

BROKEN KNITTING NEEDLE OR PAINTBRUSH

Parts list

Diode type OA90
220pF capacitor
Three pins
Crystal earpiece with plug
Miniature socket ("break contact" chassis type) to fit plug on earpiece
3m electric wire for the earth
15m electric wire for the aerial
Veroboard 9 tracks × 12 holes

To make the tuning coil you need a piece of 9mm diameter ferrite rod, about 10cm long,

and 3m of enamelled copper wire, size s.w.g. 32.

You can probably find the other things you need around the house:
Piece of thick paper 57mm × 80mm
Short piece of knitting needle or thin paintbrush handle
"Araldite" or other strong epoxy resin glue
Paper glue and sticky tape
Thread and thin needle

Making the tuning coil and rod

1

Roll the paper once round the ferrite rod and mark where the edge of the paper first touches itself.

2

MARK

Cover the paper from the mark to the far edge with glue. Put the rod back on the unglued part.

3

ROLL UP

Roll paper to make a tube round the rod. Make sure rod slides easily in the tube. Remove rod.

4

TAPE WIRE NEAR END OF TUBE

Now you have to wind the copper wire round the tube. About 8cm from the end of the wire, tape it to the tube to hold it in place.

5

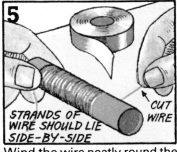

STRANDS OF WIRE SHOULD LIE SIDE-BY-SIDE

CUT WIRE

Wind the wire neatly round the tube exactly 70 times, then cover all the wire with clear sticky tape. Cut the wire about 8cm from the tube.

6

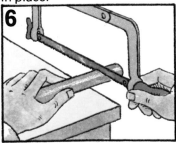

Saw a groove round the rod, 20mm from one end, then hold it in a rag and press it over a table edge to break it.

7

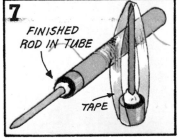

FINISHED ROD IN TUBE

TAPE

Glue a piece of knitting needle, or paintbrush, to one end of the rod. Support it with tape for several hours until it is dry.*

*Read the instructions for your glue to see how long it takes. 39

Building the circuit

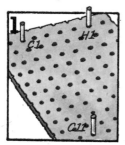

Cut the board and draw a grid with tracks vertical. Solder the pins in C1, H1 and C11.

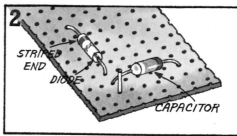

Put the diode in holes C4 and C9, with the striped end nearest C4. The capacitor goes in holes C10 and H10, and it does not matter which leg goes in which hole.

Break the track in hole C6 with a drill bit.

Now hold the socket* with the nut on the right and the terminals on top, as shown in the picture. Solder two wires about 5cm long to the two terminals nearest you. Solder the other ends of the wires to pins C1 and H1.

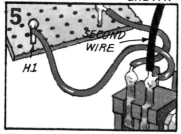

Then solder a second short wire to the socket terminal which is wired to pin H1, as shown above.

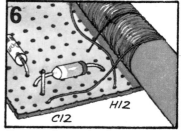

Scrape the ends of the copper wire with a knife to remove the thin coating. Solder the wires in C12 and H12. Tie tube to board using a needle and thread.

Making the aerial

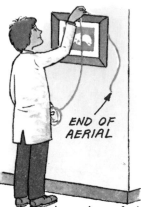

END OF AERIAL

DANGLE END OF AERIAL OUT OF WINDOW

The aerial is a long piece of wire which picks up the radio signals. The quality of the sound from the radio depends on how good the aerial is.

To make the aerial, solder one end of the 15m electric wire* to pin C11. Leaving the radio where it is, unwind the rest of the aerial wire and lay it out straight. It is best if you put the free end of the aerial somewhere high, as shown in the pictures. You may have to experiment to find the best place after you have tuned the radio (see next page).

END OF AERIAL

1 The earth

CROCODILE CLIP

EARTH WIRE

To make an earth for the radio, attach one end of the 3m piece of wire to a tap. You can use a crocodile clip, or strip the wire and wind it round the tap.

2

CONNECTION

SOCKET

Connect the other end of the earth wire to the loose piece of wire hanging from the miniature socket on the radio.

*If you live in a place with poor radio reception you may need a longer aerial

41

Tuning the radio

Now, if you have connected the earth and the aerial, you are ready to tune in.

TUNING ROD   AERIAL

Plug the earpiece into the socket and slide the ferrite rod into the tube. Then put the earpiece in your ear and very slowly slide the rod up and down inside the tube. You should hear several stations as you move the tuning rod.

If the sound is not very good, try moving the aerial to a different place. If the radio does not work at all, make sure all the joints are firm, check the earth connection and wiggle the earpiece plug in the socket to make sure it is firm.

More circuits for the radio

On the next few pages you can find out how to build an amplifier and a loudspeaker for the radio.

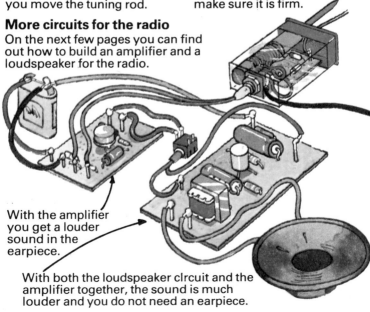

With the amplifier you get a louder sound in the earpiece.

With both the loudspeaker circuit and the amplifier together, the sound is much louder and you do not need an earpiece.

Amplifier for the radio

The amplifier makes the radio signals stronger, and this is why the sound from the earpiece is louder with the amplifier.

Parts list

1.5KΩ resistor (brown, green, red)
2.7KΩ resistor (red, violet, red)
4.7KΩ resistor (yellow, violet, red)
330KΩ resistor (orange, orange, yellow)

2.2µF electrolytic capacitor
Transistor type BFY52
Chassis socket ("break contact" type) and plug
Six pins and some electric wire
Veroboard 11 tracks x 14 holes
4.5 volt battery

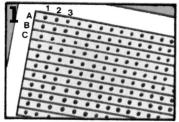

Cut the Veroboard to size and draw a grid with the tracks horizontal. Label the tracks A–K and the holes 1–14.

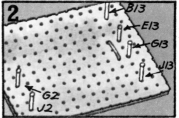

Solder the six pins in holes G2, J2, B13, E13, G13 and J13. Then solder a short wire link from E12 to G12.

Next, solder the four resistors in position as shown on the right. The brown, green, red resistor (1.5KΩ) goes in B4, F4. The red, violet, red one (2.7KΩ) goes in G4, J4. The yellow, violet, red one (4.7KΩ) goes in B11, E11 and the orange, orange, yellow resistor goes in F11, J11.

*If you have a different kind of socket, see page 60.

4 GROOVE

The capacitor has a groove and a + sign at one end. Put the leg on that end in hole B10 and the other leg in B5.

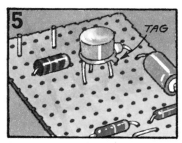

5 TAG

The transistor goes in holes E6, F5 and G6, and the leg nearest the tag should be in hole E6. Then break the track in holes B8 and G9.

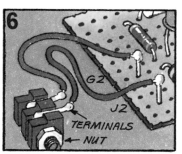

6 G2 J2 TERMINALS NUT

Solder two wires to pins G2 and J2. Hold the socket* with the nut facing you. Solder the wires to the terminals on the right.

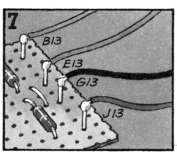

7 B13 E13 G13 J13

Then solder four more wires, each about 8cm long, to the four pins on the other edge of the board.

Fixing the amplifier to the radio

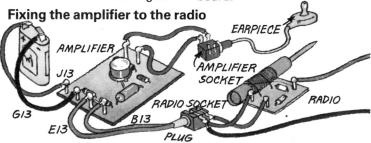

EARPIECE
AMPLIFIER
J13
AMPLIFIER SOCKET
RADIO SOCKET
RADIO
G13
E13
B13
PLUG

Unscrew the plastic case of the plug. Thread the B13 and E13 wires through the case, then solder them to the terminals on the plug. Put the plug in the socket on the radio. Connect wire G13 to the negative battery terminal and J13 to the positive terminal. Put the earpiece plug in the amplifier socket. Tune in.

44 *If you have a different kind of socket, see page 60.*

How to build the loudspeaker unit

If you build this circuit and connect it to the radio, you can listen to the radio without an earpiece. You will need to build the amplifier circuit on the previous two pages as well, though, as the loudspeaker unit will not work without it.

When you have built all three circuits it is a good idea to label all the wires, so you know which wire is which, and how to connect them.

Parts list

82Ω resistor (grey, red, black)
15KΩ resistor (brown, green, orange)
39KΩ resistor (orange, white, orange)
Two 47µF electrolytic capacitors
Transistor type AC141
Audio transformer type LT700
8Ω miniature loudspeaker
Plug to fit amplifier socket
Five pins
Some electric wire
Veroboard 13 tracks x 20 holes

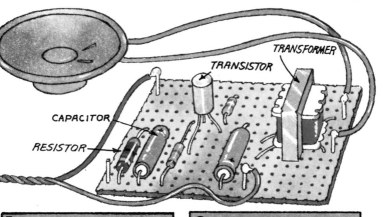

Draw a grid with the tracks horizontal. Solder the five pins in holes B1, M1, M13, D20 and H20.

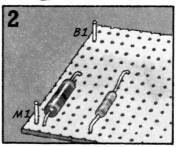

The grey, red, black resistor (82Ω) goes in F2 and M2 and the brown, green, orange one (15KΩ) in E6, M6.

45

Each capacitor has a groove and a + sign on its positive end. Put one capacitor in holes F4 and M4, with the positive leg in F4.

Put the other capacitor in E11 and M11, with its positive leg in M11. Then put the orange, white, orange (39KΩ) resistor in B9, E9. Break the track in hole M9.

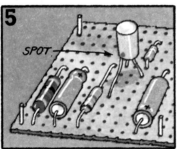

The transistor goes in E7, I7 and F9. Be careful to put the leg nearest the spot (or tag) in I7 and the centre leg in E7.

Bend the two thick legs of the audio transformer up flat under it. Then put the wire legs in B13, G13, I13, D19 and H19.

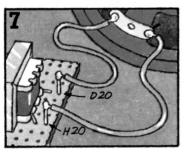

Solder two wires, about 8cm long, to pins D20 and H20. Solder the other ends of the wires to the loudspeaker.

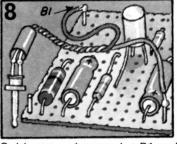

Solder two wires to pins B1 and M13. Unscrew the cap on the plug, thread wires through it and solder to plug terminals.

Setting up the loudspeaker

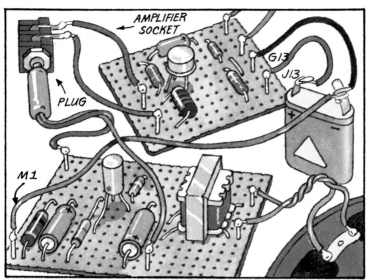

Fit the loudspeaker unit plug into the amplifier socket. Connect amplifier wire G13 to the negative battery terminal and the J13 wire to the positive terminal.

Then connect the negative battery terminal to pin M1 on the loudspeaker with another piece of wire. Connect radio to amplifier as shown on page 44.

If the loudspeaker does not work, undo the cover of the plug (see picture 8) and resolder the wires the other way round.

More about components
Resistors

Resistors are one of the most common components in a piece of electronic equipment. They are used to control and reduce the current in a circuit.

Inside a resistor there is a substance, usually carbon, through which it is difficult for the electrons to flow. The carbon is said to resist the flow of electrons, and this is how the resistor reduces the current.

Fixed resistors

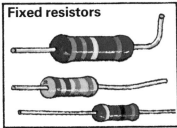

These are made in lots of different amounts of resistance. The coloured stripes on each resistor show how strong it is and this colour code is explained on the opposite page.

Variable resistors

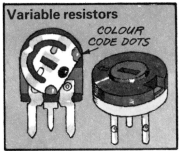

COLOUR CODE DOTS

The resistance of these resistors can be adjusted by turning the screw in the middle. They are also called potentiometers.

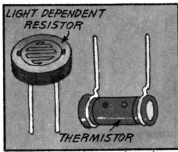

LIGHT DEPENDENT RESISTOR

THERMISTOR

A light dependent resistor has a high resistance in the dark and low resistance in the light. A thermistor changes its resistance when it is heated.

Circuit symbols for resistors

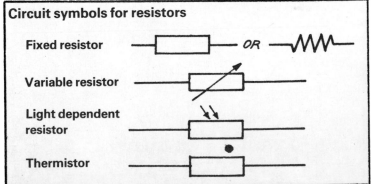

48

Resistor colour code

The three coloured stripes on one end of the resistor show its resistance and the chart on the right shows what each of the colours stands for. Each resistor also has a gold, silver, red, or brown stripe at the other end.

Resistance is measured in ohms and the colours of the first two stripes give the first two figures in the number of ohms. The colour of the third stripe shows how many noughts you should add to the number. The pictures below show you how to read the stripes on a resistor.

Colour		Number or No. of 0s
	Black	0
	Brown	1
	Red	2
	Orange	3
	Yellow	4
	Green	5
	Blue	6
	Violet	7
	Grey	8
	White	9

Reading the stripes

COLOUR CODE STRIPES

GOLD STRIPE

Hold the resistor so the three stripes of the colour code are on the left and the other stripe is on the right. Then read the colours from left to right.

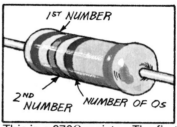

1ST NUMBER

2ND NUMBER   NUMBER OF 0s

This is a 270Ω resistor. The first stripe is red which stands for 2. The second stripe is violet which is 7 and the third stripe, brown, shows that the number has one nought.

Variable resistor

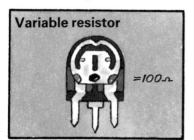

=100Ω

The maximum resistance of a variable resistor is sometimes shown by three coloured dots which you read in the same way as for fixed resistors.

Puzzle

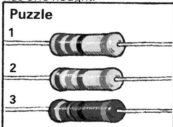

1

2

3

Can you work out the colour code on these three resistors? The answers are on the last page of this book.

Resistor experiments

Here are some tests you can do with resistors to see how they reduce the current in a circuit. You will need a 10Ω, a 15Ω, an 18Ω, and a 22Ω resistor for the fixed resistor test, and a 100Ω variable resistor for the other test.

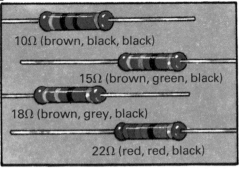

10Ω (brown, black, black)

15Ω (brown, green, black)

18Ω (brown, grey, black)

22Ω (red, red, black)

These are the resistors you will need for the fixed resistor test below.

Fixed resistor test

For this test you need a 3.5V lamp and a 4.5V battery. Connect the four resistors to the lamp and battery as shown in the picture below. The free wire coming from the battery is called a wander lead. Touch each of the resistors in turn with the wander lead and see what happens to the light from the lamp.

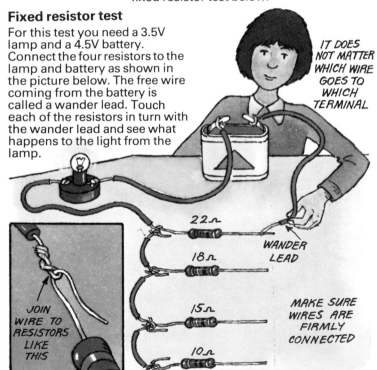

IT DOES NOT MATTER WHICH WIRE GOES TO WHICH TERMINAL

22Ω

18Ω

15Ω

10Ω

WANDER LEAD

JOIN WIRE TO RESISTORS LIKE THIS

MAKE SURE WIRES ARE FIRMLY CONNECTED

Each time you touch a resistor you make a circuit through it for the current. The bulb is dimmer with the higher value resistors because they resist the current more than the lower value ones.

What resistors do

The current in a circuit is a bit like water in a hosepipe. If you step on the pipe you reduce the flow of the water both before and after your foot. A resistor has the same effect as your foot on the hosepipe. It reduces the flow of the current through the whole of the circuit.

Resistor circuits

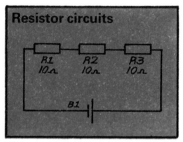

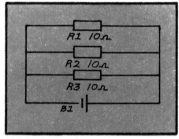

When you connect three 10Ω resistors together like this, in a series circuit, you get a total of 30Ω resistance in the circuit.

With the resistors in parallel though, there is less resistance in the circuit. With three 10Ω resistors, like this, there is only 3.3Ω resistance.

Variable resistor test

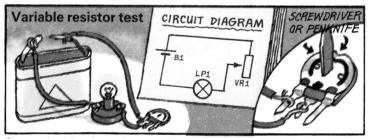

Set up the circuit as shown above, with a 4.5V battery, a 6V lamp and a 100Ω variable resistor. Join either of the wires to the centre leg of the resistor and the other wire to one of the outside legs. Turn the screw to vary the amount of resistance, and see what happens to the lamp.

How diodes work

Below there are some tests you can do to see how diodes work. For these tests you need a 4.5V battery, a 6V lamp and a diode type IN4002. For the LED test on the opposite page you need a 1.5V battery and an LED

Current can flow only one way through diodes, and they always have a stripe or arrow on one end to show you how to connect them.

Diode tests

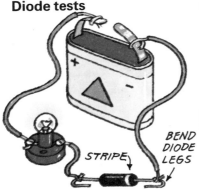

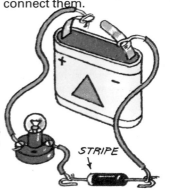

First set up the circuit as on the left, with the leg on the striped end of the diode connected to the negative battery terminal. Does the lamp light up? (It should.) Then turn the diode round so the striped end is connected to the positive

battery terminal, via the lamp. This time the lamp does not light up. The current can flow through the diode only when the leg on the striped end is connected to the negative terminal.

Circuit symbol

The arrow shows which way to place the striped end of the diode.

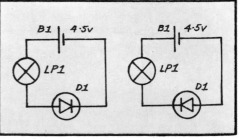

These are the circuit diagrams for the two test circuits shown above. When the arrow on the symbol points towards the negative terminal, the diode lets current flow.

Light emitting diodes

Light emitting diodes, or LEDs, are a special kind of diode which glow like tiny bulbs. LEDs are often used in calculators to light up the numbers. Like diodes, the current can flow only one way through an LED. Below you can find out how to recognize the negative leg.

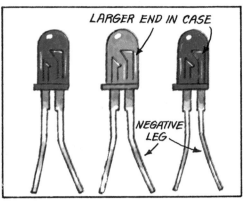

LARGER END IN CASE

NEGATIVE LEG

Finding the negative leg

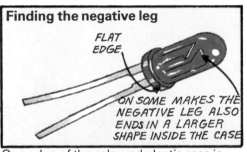

FLAT EDGE

ON SOME MAKES THE NEGATIVE LEG ALSO ENDS IN A LARGER SHAPE INSIDE THE CASE

One edge of the coloured plastic case is slightly flattened at the base. You have to look carefully to see it. The negative leg is the one next to the flat edge. If you cannot find the flat edge, you can do the test below.

Circuit symbol

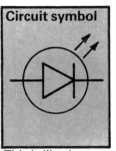

This is like the symbol for a diode, but with little arrows as well.

LED test

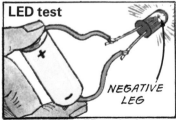

NEGATIVE LEG

Connect the LED to the battery as shown in the picture. The wire from the negative leg should be on the flat end of the battery. Does the LED light up?

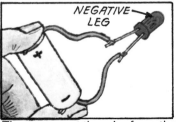

NEGATIVE LEG

Then connect the wire from the negative leg to the positive battery terminal. This time the LED does not light up. Current cannot flow through it when it is connected this way.

53

How transistors work

Transistors are very useful components. They can be used to control the strength of the current, and they can also act like a switch, turning the current off and on. They are one of the main components in transistor radios which are named after them.

Here is a circuit you can build to see how a transistor works. You will need a 4.5V battery, two 3.5V lamps and lamp holders and a transistor type BFY50.

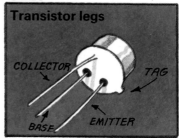

Transistor legs

COLLECTOR
TAG
BASE
EMITTER

The legs of a transistor are called "collector", "emitter" and "base". The centre leg is usually the base. You can find out how to recognize the other legs on the opposite page.

Setting up the circuit

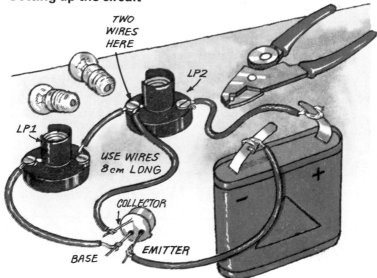

TWO WIRES HERE

LP2

LP1

USE WIRES 8 cm LONG

COLLECTOR

BASE

EMITTER

Set this circuit up very carefully and do not screw in the lamps until you are sure all the wires are connected correctly. On the BFY50 transistor, the leg nearest the tag on the case is the emitter, and it must be connected to the negative battery terminal. The base (centre leg) must be connected to lamp holder 1 and the other leg (collector) to lamp holder 2. You can fix the wires with sticky tape if you like.

Testing the circuit

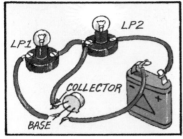

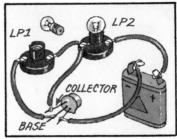

Now screw in the lamps. Lamp 1 does not light up because the current from the base leg of the transistor to the lamp is very small. The current from the collector leg to lamp 2, though, is stronger than that from the base, and lamp 2 lights up.

Try unscrewing lamp 1. There is still a circuit for the current through lamp 2 and the transistor, but lamp 2 goes out. This is because when you unscrew lamp 1, you stop the current reaching the base leg of the transistor, and this makes the transistor switch off.

Identifying transistor legs

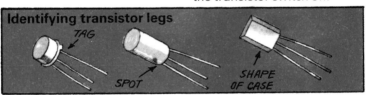

Transistors have a spot or a tag on the case, or the case may be a special shape. To identify the legs, you have to ask your supplier which leg is nearest the mark on the case. You do not need to worry about this for the projects in this book as the instructions tell you exactly where to put the legs.

Circuit symbols

The transistors used in this book are called junction transistors. There are two different kinds of junction transistors and they have slightly different symbols. One kind is called "NPN type", the other, "PNP type".

NPN type
c (COLLECTOR)
b (BASE)
e (EMITTER)

On the circuit symbol, the legs of the transistor are labelled with their initials. On an NPN type the collector must have a

PNP type
c (COLLECTOR)
b (BASE)
e (EMITTER)

positive voltage and on a PNP type the collector must have a negative voltage.

Boxing the projects

Here are some hints and ideas for how to box the projects. You need to decide how you are going to box a project before you build it. You may need to lengthen the legs of LEDs as shown on page 22. Also, any wires you plan to have coming out of the box need to be threaded through the box before you solder them to the circuit board. You can paint plastic boxes with acrylic or enamel paint.

FOOD CONTAINER
SOAP BOX
MARGARINE TUB
SPICE BOXES

There are lots of suitable, ready-made boxes you can use. Plastic, wood or stiff card ones are better than tins which are more difficult to make holes in.

Holes for wires

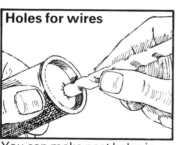

You can make neat holes in plastic or cardboard boxes with a drill bit held in your fingers. Stuff paper in the box to support it while you drill.

Tins

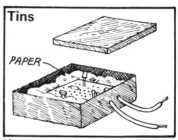

PAPER

If you use a tin, pad it with crumpled paper so the circuit board does not touch the metal. Make holes with a proper drill and smooth them with a file.

Fixing a loudspeaker

SLOTS

If the loudspeaker is to go inside the box you need to cut slots in the lid for the sound to come out. Cut the slots with a sharp knife.

Then put strong glue on the rim of the loudspeaker and stick it over the slots, on the inside of the lid.

1 Miniature radio

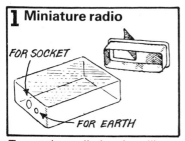

To put the radio in a box like this, make two holes in the end of the box, as shown opposite. The tuning rod and aerial wire come out of the hole in the lid.

2

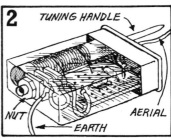

Take the nut off the socket and slide the circuit board into the box. Put the end of the socket through the hole in the box and do the nut up on the outside.

Shaky hand game

You need to make holes in the box for the metal loop and handle. Put the ends of the loop and the wire for the handle through the holes before soldering them to the board.

Pot plant tester

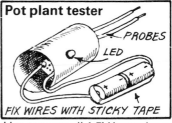

Use two small 1.5V batteries so they fit in a small box. Tape the batteries together with the positive end of one on the negative end of the other.

1 Guessing game

You need a hole for each of the LEDs and one for the wires for the switch. If you use a firm box, such as a soap box, you can put the switch in the lid.

2

To fix the switch, unscrew the collar on the switch, put the pushbutton through a hole in the lid. Then screw the collar on again.

Circuit diagrams for the projects

These are the circuit diagrams for the projects in this book. Each diagram shows how the components for that project are linked together. The components are labelled with their initials, number, and type or strength. The diagrams do not show the layout of the components on the Veroboard, only how the current flows along the tracks to each component.

New symbols

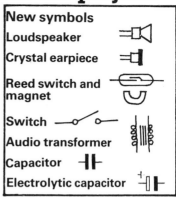

Loudspeaker

Crystal earpiece

Reed switch and magnet

Switch

Audio transformer

Capacitor

Electrolytic capacitor

Shaky hand game

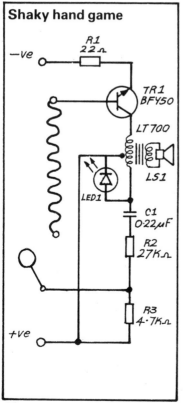

−ve

R1 22Ω

TR1 BFY50

LT 700

LED1

LS1

C1 0·22μF

R2 27KΩ

R3 4·7KΩ

+ve

Pot plant tester

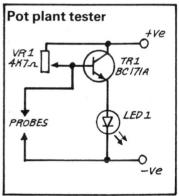

+ve

VR1 4K7Ω

TR1 BC171A

PROBES

LED1

−ve

Miniature radio

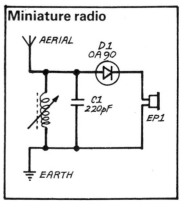

AERIAL

D1 OA90

C1 220pF

EP1

EARTH

Burglar alarm

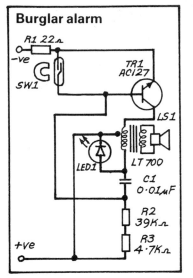

R1 22Ω
−ve
SW1
TR1 AC127
LS1
LT 700
LED1
C1 0·01μF
R2 39KΩ
R3 4·7KΩ
+ve

Guessing game

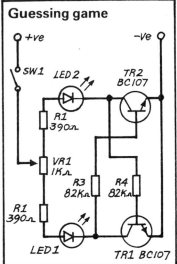

+ve
−ve
SW1
LED 2
TR2 BC107
R1 390Ω
VR1 1KΩ
R3 82KΩ
R4 82KΩ
R1 390Ω
LED1
TR1 BC107

Radio amplifier

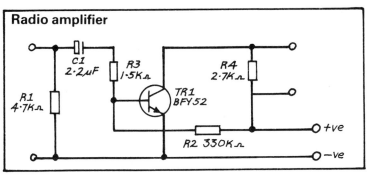

C1 2·2μF
R3 1·5KΩ
R4 2·7KΩ
R1 4·7KΩ
TR1 BFY52
R2 330KΩ
+ve
−ve

Loudspeaker unit

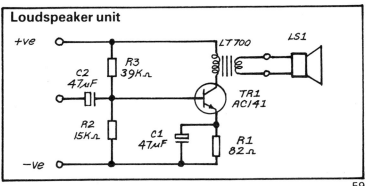

+ve
LT 700
LS1
C2 47μF
R3 39KΩ
TR1 AC141
R2 15KΩ
C1 47μF
R1 82Ω
−ve

Buying components

You can buy components in an electronics components shop, or send off for them to an electronics supplier. To find the address of a supplier, look in the advertisements in electronics hobby magazines, or ask in your local T.V. repair shop. Opposite, there is a list of all the components you will need for all the projects and tests in the book, arranged by type of component (one of each of the things with a star is for the tests). If you do not want to buy all the components at once, you will need to make your own list.

Making a list

To buy the components for only a few of the projects, copy out the parts lists given at the beginning of the projects you want to build. Check which of the things you can buy in general electrical or hardware stores (see opposite), then make a list of all the things you need to get from an electronics components supplier. Arrange your list by type of component, i.e. list all the resistors together, all the transistors, etc., and say that all the components are for use with a 4.5V or a 9V battery. State also that the Veroboard should be size 0.1in, and that you prefer "⅓ - ½ watt" resistors, and LEDs with capsule diameter 5mm.* When you go to a shop, it is a good idea to take this book with you, so they can see what you want.

Sending away for components

If you send away for the components it is a good idea to order them all at once (it will be quite costly though), as most mail order companies have a minimum charge. Copy out the list of components very carefully. Send the list with a stamped, self-addressed envelope and the supplier will reply telling you how much the order costs. They will not send the components until you send them the money.

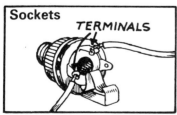

Sockets

If you have a socket which looks like this, attach the wires to the two terminals as shown in the picture.

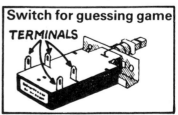

Switch for guessing game

If your switch is not like the one in the pictures, connect the battery, then try the wire on each of the terminals while pressing the switch.

*These are the best sizes for the projects, but other sizes will work as well.

List of all the components for all the projects

Resistors
(⅓ - ½ watt are best)

10Ω*
15Ω*
18Ω*
22Ω (three)*
82Ω
390Ω (two)*
1.5KΩ
2.7KΩ
4.7KΩ (three)
15KΩ
27KΩ
39KΩ (two)
82KΩ (two)
330KΩ

Variable resistors
("vertical skeleton" type)

100Ω*
1KΩ
4.7KΩ

Transistors

BC107 (two)
AC127
BFY50 (two)*
BC171A
BFY52
AC141

Diodes

OA90
IN4002*

Light emitting diodes
(capsule diameter 5mm)

5 (any colour)*

Capacitors
220pF
0.01μF
0.22μF

Electrolytic capacitors
2.2μF
47μF (two)

Audio transformer
LT 700 (three)

Reed switch (normally open type)
50cm tinned copper wire s.w.g. 20
3m enamelled copper wire s.w.g. 32
30cm plastic sleeving 2mm bore
10cm of 9mm diameter ferrite rod
Crystal earpiece and plug
Two miniature chassis sockets
    (break contact type) to fit plug on
    earpiece
Miniature plug to fit chassis socket
Veroboard with copper strips, size
    0.1in, sufficient for the following
    pieces (given as no. of
    tracks × no. of holes):
    13×15, 7×12, 14×30, 20×27,
    9×12, 11×14, 13×20
8Ω miniature loudspeaker (three of
    the projects need one of these —
    you can use the same one for all
    of them, or buy three)
Three battery clip connectors for
    9V battery

Other things you need
(You can buy the things listed below in general electrical or
hardware stores.)

Soldering iron
Cored solder
Very small screwdriver
Miniature pliers
Wire cutters
Wire strippers
25m thin electric wire (18m of this
    is for the radio). "Bell wire" or
    seven stranded wire is best, but
    thicker wire will do.
Pushbutton switch
9 volt battery
4.5 volt battery

1.5 volt battery   ⎫
Two 3.5 volt bulbs   for the
Two 6 volt bulbs   ⎬ tests
Two miniature bulb   only
    holders   ⎭
Magnet (any kind)
Clear sticky tape
"Araldite" (or other type of epoxy
    resin glue)
Paper glue
Metal paperclips (to use as
    "pins" — see page 21)

One of each of the things with a star is for the tests.

Hints on identifying components

The components you buy will probably all be mixed up together and it is quite a job to identify them and work out which ones to use for each project.

   The first thing to do is to sort them into different types, that is, put all the resistors together, all the transistors, etc. The pictures below should help you do this.* One or two of your components, though, may not look like any of those in the pictures. If you cannot identify them, first sort out all the rest of the components and work out which ones are for which project (there are some hints to help you on the opposite page). Then you should be able to identify the last few components by seeing which ones you are missing.

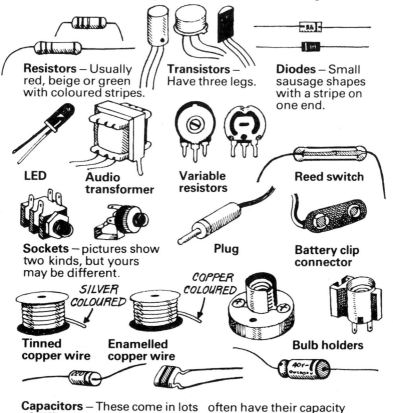

Resistors – Usually red, beige or green with coloured stripes.

Transistors – Have three legs.

Diodes – Small sausage shapes with a stripe on one end.

LED

Audio transformer

Variable resistors

Reed switch

Sockets – pictures show two kinds, but yours may be different.

Plug

Battery clip connector

SILVER COLOURED

COPPER COLOURED

Tinned copper wire

Enamelled copper wire

Bulb holders

Capacitors – These come in lots of different shapes, sizes and colours. Have two legs and often have their capacity printed on them in numbers.

*None of the things are shown to scale.

Finding the right components for each project

The components you need for each project are given in the parts list at the beginning of the project. Some components have their type number or strength printed on them in very small numbers, so a magnifying glass is useful for identifying them. Sometimes the numbers are printed amongst a lot of other numbers and the signs for ohms (Ω), microfarads (μF) and picofarads (pF) are left off, so you have to look carefully to spot the numbers. Here are some clues to help you identify the components for each project.

Resistors

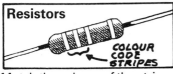

COLOUR CODE STRIPES

Match the colours of the stripes with the colours given for the resistors in the parts lists. For how to read the stripes, see page 15.

Variable resistors

Look for figures, which are numbers of ohms (N.B. 4.7KΩ is sometimes written 4K7), or for dots of colour from the resistor colour code (see page 49).

Transistors

Look for the type number printed on the case. Be careful as the numbers rub off easily.

Diodes

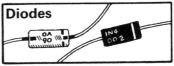

Look carefully to find the type number which is usually printed on the case.

Capacitors

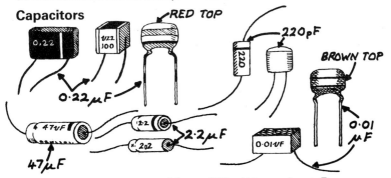

This picture shows some of the different kinds, but yours may not look like any of these. Most of them, though, will probably have numbers on them showing their capacitance. Some of the numbers are quite difficult to work out. For instance, $2\mu2$ means 2.2μF and $\frac{\mu22}{100}$ means 0.22μF. If some of your capacitors have stripes, the one with a brown top is 0.01μF and the one with a red top is 0.22μF

Faults checklist

If one of your projects is not working, check through this list of possible faults to see what could be wrong. The most likely things are at the top of the list. In electronics you often have to check a board several times before you get the circuit to work.

MAKE SURE THE BATTERY IS NOT FLAT

1 Check very carefully to make sure *all* the components, pins and wire links, are in the correct holes.

2 Make sure that transistors, diodes and electrolytic capacitors are the right way round. If any are wrong, resolder them the right way. If the circuit still does not work, use new components of the same type.

3 Make sure the wires from the board to the battery are correctly connected to the positive and negative battery terminals. If they were wrong, correct them, then test the circuit. If it still does not work, try replacing the transistors, electrolytic capacitors, diodes and LEDs.

4 There should be no bits of wire, or components' legs, touching each other on the plainside of the board.

5 Have you remembered to drill out the holes in the tracks?

6 Make sure there is no solder between the tracks. If there is, remove it by running the bit of the soldering iron along in the groove between the tracks.

7 Check the soldered joints. They should all be shiny and firm. If they are not, resolder them.

8 Examine the tracks to make sure they are all still firmly stuck to the board. If a piece of track has come unstuck, or broken, solder a piece of wire across it, as shown in the picture below.

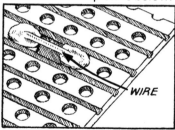

WIRE

9 If the circuit still does not work, the transistors may be damaged. Replace them with new transistors of the same type.

10 If, after checking all these points and correcting any faults, the circuit still does not work, send it to us and we will see if we can find out what is wrong. Wrap it up carefully and send it (with a stamp for our reply) to: Electronics Adviser, Usborne Publishing, 20 Garrick Street, London WC2E 9BJ, England.